STEPNEY

Based on *The Railway Series* by the Rev. W. Awdry

Illustrations by
Robin Davies and Jerry Smith

EGMONT

EGMONT

We bring stories to life

First published in Great Britain in 2004
by Egmont UK Limited
239 Kensington High Street, London W8 6SA
This edition published in 2008
All Rights Reserved

ISBN 978 1 4052 3466 5
1 3 5 7 9 10 8 6 4 2
Printed in Italy

TO THE TRAINS ➡️

This is a story about Stepney, the Bluebell Engine. One day I sent him to work with Mavis and Toby at the Quarry. I told him to leave there before it got dark, but he didn't listen to me ...

Stepney usually worked with his friend Rusty. But one day, The Fat Controller said, "I hear you could do with a change of scene, so I want you to help Toby and Mavis at the Quarry."

"Thank you, Sir," Stepney said. "Shall I be away for long?"

"Just today," said The Fat Controller. "And make sure you leave the Quarry before it gets dark. It's very easy to get lost up there."

Stepney soon arrived at the Quarry. Toby and Mavis were waiting for him.

"We're glad you're here to help," said Toby. "We have a lot of work to do."

"Are those my trucks?" asked Stepney.

"Some of them," said Mavis. "There are lots more waiting in the sidings."

"The more the merrier," said Stepney happily.

Stepney really enjoyed working with Mavis and Toby. Later that day, the Quarry Foreman spoke to Stepney's Driver.

"Do you want to take a night special to the building site on the new branch line?" he asked.

"Yes, please," said Stepney's Driver. He had forgotten The Fat Controller's warning about how easy it was to get lost up there in the dark.

Soon night came.

"Be careful, Stepney," said Toby. "It gets very dark on the hillside tracks."

"I will," said Stepney. "Thank you for a lovely day. I do hope I can come back again, soon."

"Watch out," said Mavis. "The line can be rather spooky at night!"

"Thanks for the warning," said Stepney as he puffed away.

Stepney made the delivery. Once everything had been unloaded he set off for home.

That was when the trouble began. It was very foggy, so Stepney could hardly see where he was going.

"Mavis was right," he said nervously. "Suddenly everything does look rather spooky!"

"There's a signalbox ahead," said his Driver. "The signal is turned to green so someone must be expecting us."

But the points had been accidentally set in the wrong direction. Stepney and his Driver didn't realise that, so they carried on down the wrong track. After a while they realised they didn't know where they were.

"We're lost!" said Stepney's Driver. "I think we should wait here until the fog clears."

Suddenly, they heard a noise.
"What was that?" said Stepney nervously.

As the fog cleared, they realised they were in the scrap yard! Stepney's Driver and Firemen went to find the Foreman.

Two diesels approached Stepney.
"You'll make good scrap, Stepney," they said.

"Help!" cried Stepney, but no one heard him.

The diesels took Stepney to a smelters shed. "Goodbye, Stepney," they said.

Stepney looked up nervously. There was a huge grabber moving down towards him.
"But I'm not meant to be scrapped!" he cried.

"It's too late now," said the diesels.

But just as the machine was about to grab him, it suddenly stopped. The Fat Controller had turned it off. He had saved Stepney!

"Oh! Thank you, Sir," said Stepney gratefully.

"You are very lucky that I decided to visit this yard tonight," said The Fat Controller sternly. "I can't always be around to save you, Stepney. You have to be more careful!"

Stepney promised to always listen to warnings from then on.

Stepney's Driver was in trouble, too. He had agreed to do the night job without asking The Fat Controller first.

He was very sorry for the trouble he had caused. He promised he would always ask The Fat Controller in future before taking on any jobs.

"I have learnt something useful from this," said Stepney.

"What's that?" asked The Fat Controller.

"I've learnt that there's no place like home!" Stepney said.

"That's very true," said The Fat Controller. "And that's where you are going now."

When Stepney got back to the station, he told Rusty all about his scary time on the foggy hillside and his near-miss at the scrap yard.

Even though it had been exciting to work somewhere different for a while, Stepney realised he was happiest working on The Fat Controller's railway with his good friend, Rusty.

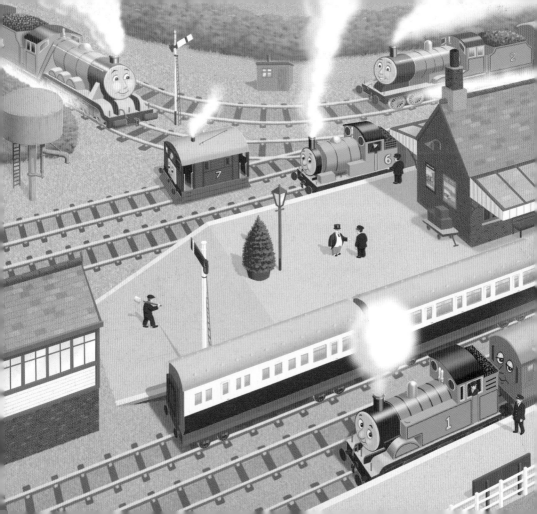

The Thomas Story Library is THE definitive collection of stories about Thomas and ALL his friends.

5 more Thomas Story Library titles will be chuffing into your local bookshop in August 2008!

Jeremy

Hector

BoCo

Billy

Whiff

And there are even more Thomas Story Library books to follow later!

So go on, start your Thomas Story Library NOW!

A Fantastic Offer for Thomas the Tank Engine Fans!

In every Thomas Story Library book like this one, you will find a special token. Collect 6 Thomas tokens and we will send you a brilliant Thomas poster, and a double-sided bedroom door hanger! Simply tape a £1 coin in the space above, and fill out the form overleaf.

Cut along the dotted line

TO BE COMPLETED BY AN ADULT

To apply for this great offer, ask an adult to complete the coupon below and send it with a pound coin and 6 tokens, to:
THOMAS OFFERS, PO BOX 715, HORSHAM RH12 5WG

☐ Please send a Thomas poster and door hanger. I enclose 6 tokens plus a £1 coin. (Price includes P&P)

Fan's name..

Address..

....Postcode...........................

Date of birth..

Name of parent/guardian...

Signature of parent/guardian...

Please allow 28 days for delivery. Offer is only available while stocks last. We reserve the right to change the terms of this offer at any time and we offer a 14 day money back guarantee. This does not affect your statutory rights.

☐ Data Protection Act: If you do not wish to receive other similar offers from us or companies we recommend, please tick this box. Offers apply to UK only.

Cut along the dotted line